JURASSIC JEFF

SPACE INVADER

Also by Royden Lepp

Rust: Visitor in the Field
Rust: Secrets of the Cell
Rust: Death of the Rocket Boy
Rust: Soul in the Machine
Rust: The Boy Soldier
David: The Shepherd's Song
Barnabas Goes Swimming
Barnabas Helps a Friend
Happy Birthday Barnabas
God Loves You Barnabas
How to Draw Good, Bad & Ugly Bible Guys
How to Draw Big Bad Bible Beasts

JURASSIC JEFF

SPACE INVADER

Jurassic Jeff: Space Invader was created with Adobe Photoshop on Wacom technology, but also with some pencils on some paper.

 Published in the United States by RH Graphic, an imprint of Random House Children's Books, a division of Penguin Random House LLC, New York.

RH Graphic with the book design is a trademark of Penguin Random House LLC.

Visit us on the web! RHKidsGraphic.com • @RHKidsGraphic

Educators and librarians, for a variety of teaching tools, visit us at RHTeachersLibrarians.com

Library of Congress Cataloging-in-Publication Data is available upon request.
ISBN 978-0-593-56539-1 (hardcover) — ISBN 978-0-593-56540-7 (library binding)
ISBN 978-0-593-56541-4 (ebook)

Designed by Patrick Crotty
Interior color assistance by Della Warren

MANUFACTURED IN CHINA
10 9 8 7 6 5 4 3 2 1
First Edition

A comic on every bookshelf.

This book is for my son, Edison.
Dragon the dragonfly was his idea.

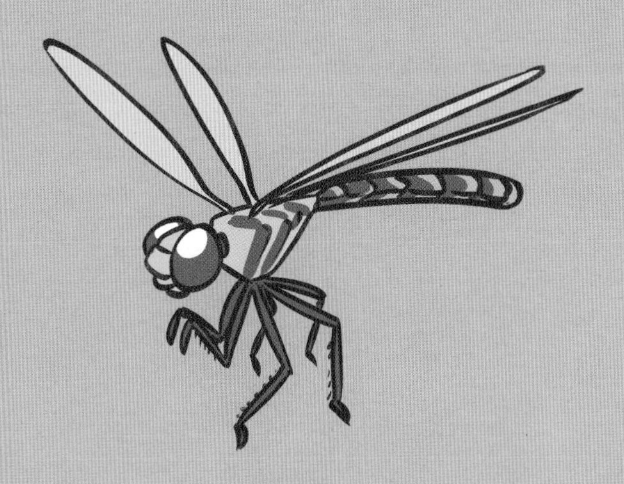

FZZZZZZZZZZZZZZZZZZZZ
POP
FTZ

CLANG

Whoooaaaaaa!!!

crack
BANG

Oh no! My WARP DRIVE!

POP
POP

Skip
Skip

WOMP

Waaaa...

Click it or ticke-

KA-

BOOM!

Hey, guys!
Check it out.

-Click-
-bZzt-

-Click-
-Click-
Hallo Erdlinge
-Click-
01100111 01110010
0110010...
-Click-
-Click-
-Click-
-Click-
Greetings...

Ha ha!
Greetings, Earthlings!

My name is ***Jeff.*** I come from the Θζπæ¤ star system. I ***do not*** come in peace. I am your new ruler...

PLIP
Plop

Ha
Ha
Ha
Ha
I am here to conquer this planet!
Please take me to your elected or self-elected ruler, mortal deity, or principal organism!

What's going on here? How old is this planet anyway?
Let's see... Earth... Third planet from star #76B...

Four billion three hundred and sixty-five million years old?!
That's way too young! They told me this mission was of utmost importance.
How did this happen?
This planet won't even have a real multitasking species for another 100 million years!

The first attempt at instant coffee is probably 65 million years away.
So are *chicken nuggets!*

There is currently **no intelligent life** on this planet!

What's a chicken nugget?
Whoa, whoa, whoa. Hold on there, my tiny green friend...
What exactly do you mean by "*intelligent*"?

I like to think that we all evolve at our own pace.
We try not to base intelligence on drool. *Spike* is a member of our family.

Well, Jeff, welcome to Earth. We're glad you came. We'd be more than happy to help you on your journey.
My name is Carl.
This is Hungry.
Hi, Jeff.
And this is Spike.

You guys would really take me to your leader?
Sure, why not? We just need to figure out... I mean...

Hungry, I was thinking Rex is kind of our "leader."
Just because Rex is bossy doesn't mean he's our leader.

Okay, fine. Who do you think our leader is?
I think Mike has leadership *skills*, but he has a long way to go before he's a leader.
I've always thought *Doug* would make a good leader.
I agree. Doug doesn't realize how respected he is as a diplodocus.
Diplodocuses lack respect. It's a fact. I have several diplodocus friends.
I think *Trevor* is a great, wise leader.
Trevor! Of course, that's where we will take him!
That's enough!

ZzZAAPP
Pop
Pop
Bzzt

Pop
Pop
Bzzt

Bz
BZTT

See? Now this doesn't seem polite.

Pop
Pop

Carl, you're flying!
I know! It tickles!
Bzzt
BZzzz

Can I be next?
Pop

Pop
Bzzzzt

SHLURRP!

Well, that answers that question.
If Spike likes you...

...you're okay with us.
I am?

Uh-oh!
That drained my space suit battery.

Is that bad?

It means that my space suit stops creating nitrogen for me to breathe.
Your Earth oxygen is poisonous to me.

I'll just replace my battery.

It should last until I overthrow your leadership and establish my dominion over Earth.

But I better not use my ray gun anymore.

Okay, we shall begin the *primary mission:*
Take me to your leader!

Actually, hang on. I should probably feed my fish, *Charles.*

Okay, now I'm ready!

All right! I think Trevor is still doing his talks down at Emerald Lake. Shall we head in that direction?
Yes! But let's go over the north pass. It's more scenic.
Scenic?

Oh yes, you're going to *love* this planet.

Jeff, look here on our left to take in the magnificent views of the green ***peaks of Kaza.***

Truly stunning in the early hours of the morning.

Is that where we're going?

Uh, no. I've never been to Kaza.

If you look to our left, you can gaze upon the misty hills of *Moví.*

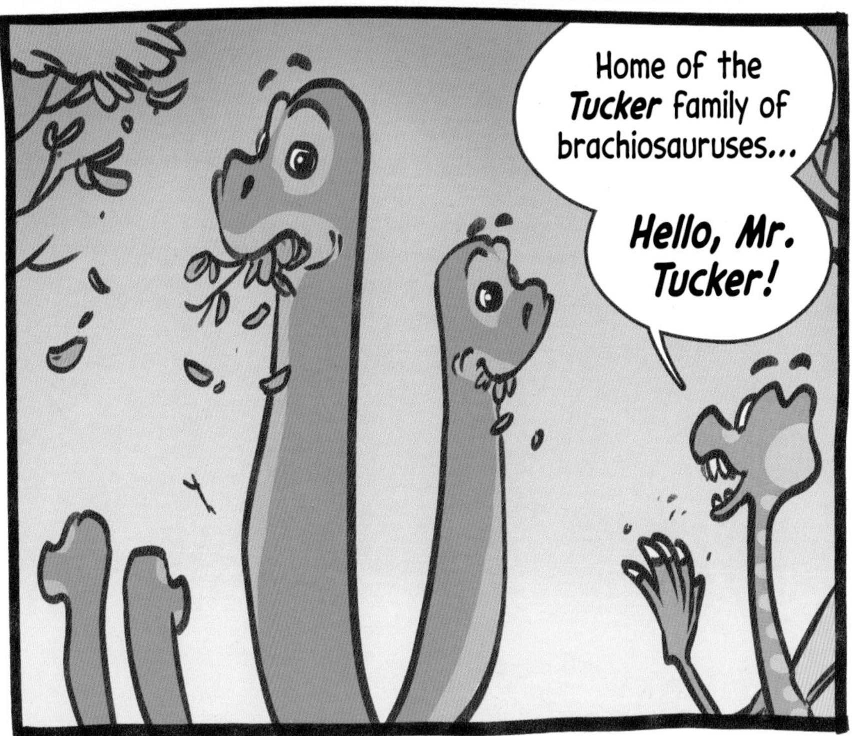
Home of the *Tucker* family of brachiosauruses...
Hello, Mr. Tucker!

Hi, Carl!

It's so nice that Carl has always befriended the...
...less popular creatures among us.

Was one of those the leader?

The Tuckers? Oh no. They're just dear friends.

Ah yes, here we are!

We have arrived?

Yes, we have!

Terra Falls Canyons!
One of the most spectacular wonders of the modern world.

Ch-cheeetz

So this is the location of your leader?

Of course not. This is just a beautiful place.

Is it on the way?

Kind of. I mean, Hungry and Spike and I always take the scenic routes.
And honestly we thought you might like to see the beauty of the planet you plan to conquer.

So that you can *appreciate* Earth.

This is incorrect! This is not what I asked for. I asked you to take me to your leader!

Appreciation of the dominated planet is not part of the mission.

What *exactly* is the mission, Jeff?

It's to show them that I'm capable...

...I mean...

It's to invade and conquer this planet!

I don't care *who* lives here. I don't care if it's *pretty.*

It's mine now!
I am the supreme ruler of Earth...

Well...?
What now?

No, *Dragon!* That is not what I asked for.

I asked you to pick up fish.
Bad dragonfly!
No treat!

Well, you ***should*** feel bad. I think I was pretty clear.

Well, that's true. ***It is green,*** but it's not a fish!

What exactly *did* you bring us?

It's not even edible.

Well, I agree. It's definitely the strangest thing I've seen today.

What an ugly little creature.

Well...
...*now* what am I going to do for dinner?

Excuse me, but did I hear you say that you required cooking?

Dragon, is the food talking to us?

You see, aside from conquering worlds, I consider myself to be somewhat of a chef.

Are you sure this is a good idea, Carl?

It does seem pretty steep.

I don't know what choice we have.

Hmm...
...we could just *leave* him.
Maybe someone else will help him complete his space mission.

Do you *really* think that someone else is going to help him?

No, he's going to get eaten.

And that would make us feel...?

We feel ***bad*** when friends get eaten.

I think Jeff just got off on the wrong foot.
I believe that there's a true friend inside that green creature that is inside that strange frozen water bubble.

But this is actually kind of dangerous.
Are we really going to risk our lives for someone who has been mean to us?

All right...

Let's let Spike decide.

Spike, do you think we should try to help our *kind-of-annoying* new friend, Jeff?

Well, that settles that. Don't mind if I do, Spike!

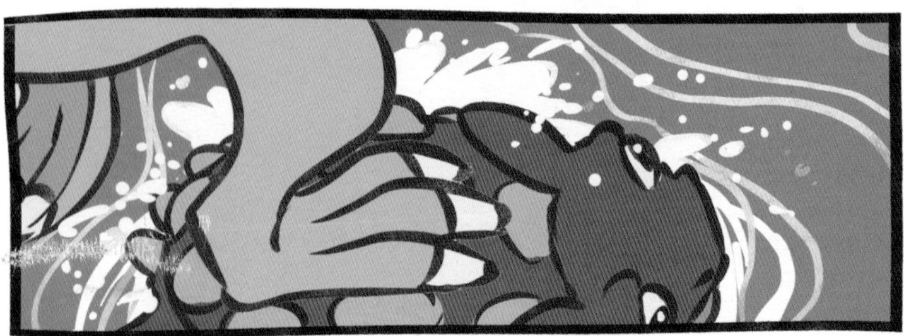

Let's go save Jeff!

Which brings me to the final three rules of cooking:

Curry stains are forever.
Peanut butter doesn't go in the fridge.

And always boil the milk of a stellar moon coconut before you cook with it. Cold lunar milk is only for cereal.

But today we want to make sure that the pastry doesn't dry out the...uh...

What kind of aquatic creature did you bring us, Dragon?

Ah yes! ***"Trout."***
You will enjoy consuming ***trout pastry*** much more than you would have enjoyed consuming me.

The key to exquisite aquatic creature pastry is knowing when to pull it out of the oven.

!?!?!

Dragon has a good point.
How *are* you going to combat the moisture?

Wonderful question, Dragon. Let's pull it out now so I can show you.

Aha! As you can see, when the skeletal structure of the aquatic creature pulls free of the pastry, *it's ready!*

What do we do with the skeletal structure?

We *discard* it!
As we no longer have any use for it.

We also don't need this ***giant tomato.***
Or this ***very rotten egg.***
But thanks for picking them up, Dragon!

!!!

What will we do if Jeff is way up on one of those things?
We'll cross that bridge when we come to it. Don't worry so much.
Dragonflies nest up high, don't they?

Did you see that?!
Whack

A fish skeleton just landed on Spike's head!

How is a fish skeleton going to help us find Jeff?

WAP

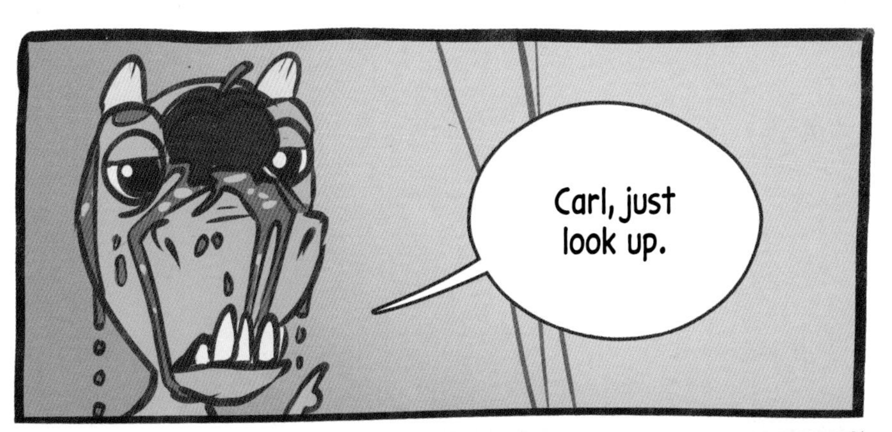
Carl, just look up.

Fine.

Oh look, it's Jeff!

Wap

Surprising, really! Absolutely fantastic!
Excellent texture and complex flavors.

So glad you like it, Sara! I'm eager to taste it myself.

Hey, Jeff!

Oh right, that other thing.

Do you still want to do that intergalactic mission?

I do! I did not forget. I'll be down in a moment.

Who is that?
Just some other lizards.
They are assisting me in conquering the planet.

Well, I must be going. I love cooking but I ***do*** have a ***primary goal*** of overthrowing this planet's leadership.

AWWWWWWWW

I know, I know. But I must be a ***responsible intergalactic invader.***
Dragon, would you be so kind?

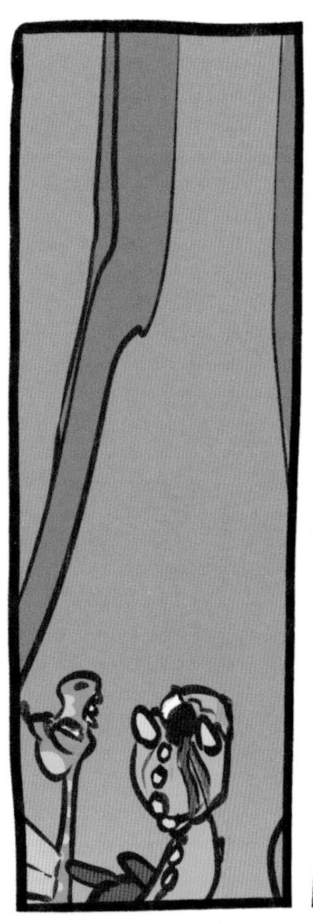

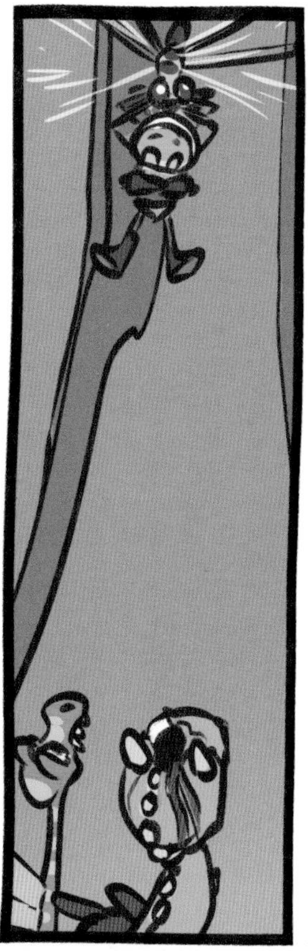

Aha! You thought I was disposed but behold: I am not.

We thought you were being *eaten.*

Of course not. Dragon here summoned me for a... *secondary mission.*

My pastry skills were required.

Now then, shall we carry on?

I imagine it's this way.

You're more than welcome to join us, Dragon. I'm going to *conquer the whole world.*
Pastry sounds *tasty.*
Hungry, you have something on your face.

Welcome to the wetlands, Jeff! We MUST cross this swamp in order to reach our great leader.
Really? What is it called?

It's called... the SWAMP of DESPAIR!

Despair?

Ah, just kidding. We don't give swamps names!

Also kidding about it being the only way. There are many more ways. This is just a pretty swamp.
It also happens to be one of the few places that grow ***the red fern.*** And Spike ***loves*** to eat red fern.
And we love Spike.

Carl, could you smack the ***swamp mosquito*** on my back? I can't reach it.

That's what friends are for!

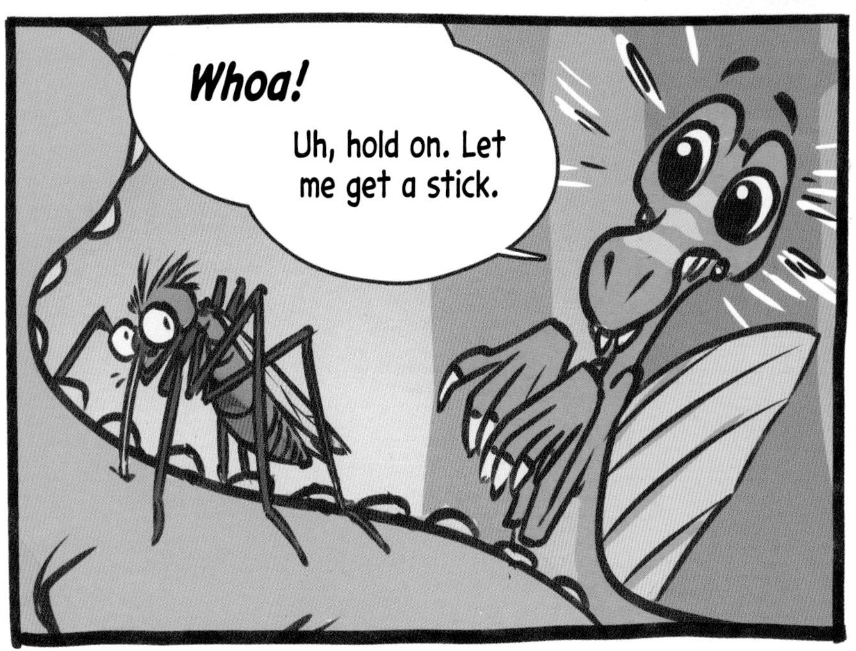
Whoa!
Uh, hold on. Let me get a stick.

Is all this *fauna* native to the swamp?

Much of it is, yes.

Thwip

The swamp animals can be a bit less friendly.

And a bit less...small?

Thwip

Fwp
Fwp
Fwp
Fwp
Fwp

Fwp Fwp Fwp Fwp Fwp

Whap
BLARF

Splat

Splort

The locals of this swamp may not have the best temperament, Jeff...

...but it really is easy to live *harmoniously* with the rest of nature.

I will teach you how to respect wildlife and learn to read the *cues* of your *surrounding ecosystem.*

For example: listen to the call of that little lizard.
Bawk Bawk

He's sending out a warning that there's a giant predator nearby.

Carl!

It's trying
to escape!

Spike!
Jeff!
Dragon!
Help!

Jeff, come grab Carl's feet!

Jeff!

What are you doing?

I have to stay focused on the goals of my mission.
I can't do any more *side quests.*

What?!
This is NOT a side quest!

Also, my academy boots say they're *water-resistant,* not *waterproof.*

Carl, can you hear me?

Yes, I can!
Hang on! We're getting you out!

I'd be happy to help you calculate the odds of success.
It's actually a pretty simple math equation.

Dragon, can you lead Spike to the front of the salamander?
I have an idea.

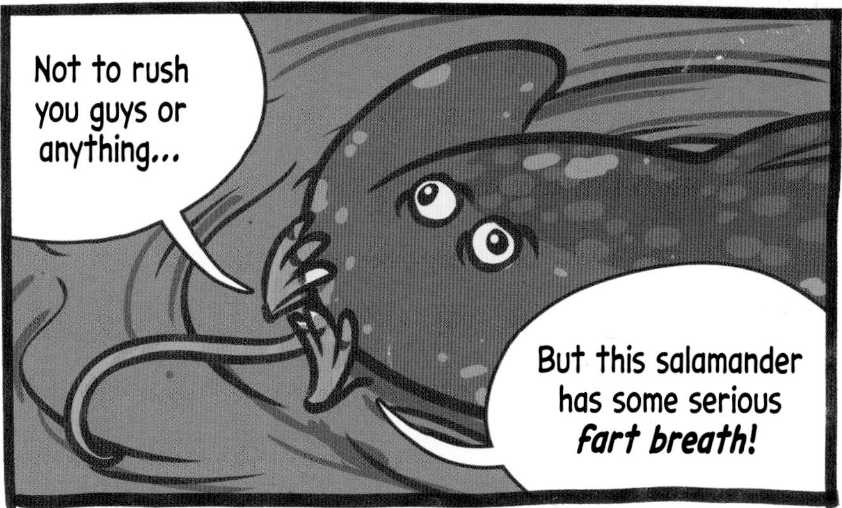
Not to rush you guys or anything...
But this salamander has some serious ***fart breath!***

Your odds of success just dropped a little!
0.01%

Okay, Carl! When you feel Spike's tail, hold on as tight as you can!
Got it!

Now, Carl!

I got him!

Hey, Spike!
Look...

...RED FERNS!

SPIOOOOP.

Very clever, my friend.
I knew you'd figure something out.

Absolutely **ZERO** thanks to ***bubble head*** over there who stood by and watched.

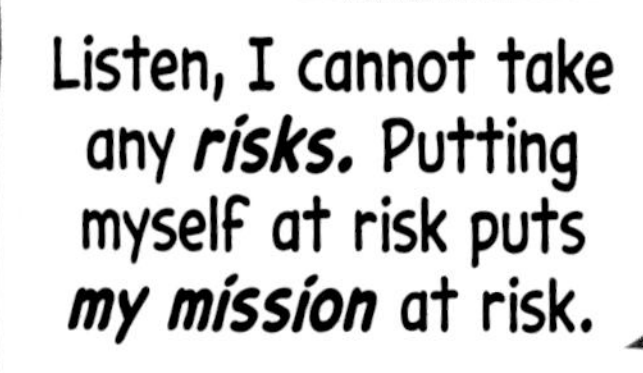

Well, then you can kiss your future chicken nuggets goodbye.

Well, you can kiss *your mission* goodbye. Go find our leader on your own.

Come on, guys.

Hey, Hungry, wait.

What's the most important thing about friendship?

That you like to eat the same stuff.

Well... That's true.
But what's ***the other*** thing?

We take care of each other's back mosquitoes?

Yes, that's also...
Well, maybe those *are* the most important things.

All right, what is the *one thing* that makes a friendship last forever?

Forgiveness.

Forgiveness.

Hey, Jeff.

I forgive you...
...for leaving me to die inside the mouth of a giant salamander with fart breath.

Hungry?

No. I don't think I need to forgive him right now.

We can still help him.

We can.

Well, that's it, then!
Shall we continue? We've made it this far, haven't we?

Yes, let's continue.

We're almost there, Jeff.

So what was your plan B for rescuing me?
Well, giant salamanders don't chew their food, so we probably would have just followed it around for the next few days until you came out the *other end.*

RING
RING

RING
RING
My phone!
I'm getting a call!

I'm getting a call from my home planet!

Hello?!

A call?

Hello? No, I can *barely* hear you.
You can barely hear me? I'm right there.

Okay, can you hear me *now?*

I can hear you right now. Will I not hear you soon?

Sorry, who is this?
Jeff, why are you talking to your square pocket rock?

Listen, I am talking ***on the phone***. I need quiet.
This is an intergalactic call.

Why don't you talk to me? I'm right here.
Sorry about that. I'm back. Who is this?

What? An extended warranty on my spaceship? I never purchased an extended...
...Look, could you tell the ***Academy of Space Exploration*** that my mission is going great and totally hasn't failed at all?

On hold? I suppose I could be put on hold for a bit but...

Can I ask a question?
CARL! I'm on ***THE PHONE.***

Look, Carl, adopting new technology is part of being ***highly evolved.*** This is how fellow cadets communicate with me.

I just need to let all the other officers know that I'm doing a great job so that they respect me and stop calling me names and stuff...

Oh, hello? Yes, just tell the academy that I definitely ***didn't*** crash, but I might need to order some parts for my ship.

...I didn't purchase the spaceship. I don't know about its warranty...
...Well, I suppose it wouldn't hurt to give you my credit card number. One moment...
...So you're going to tell the academy that I sounded really brave on the phone, right?
...Hello...?
I think he just hung up on me.
I suppose I could try to *text* him my credit card number...

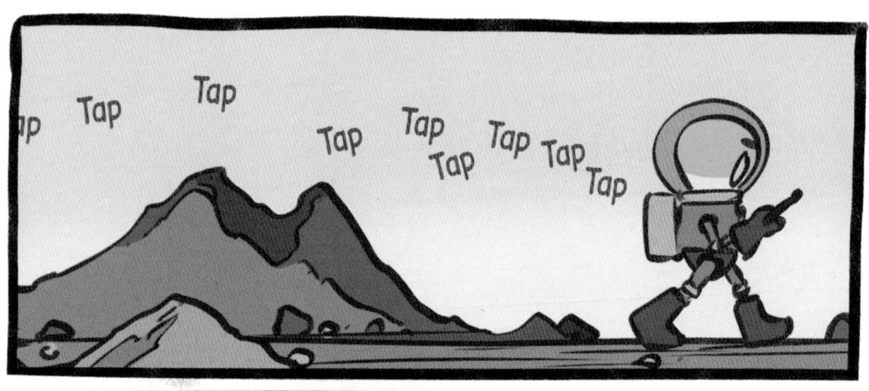
ap
Tap
Tap
Tap
Tap
Tap
Tap
Tap
Tap

Trip

AAAAAA
Tap
Tap
Tap
Tap

Rumble

Oh, hey!

It's an *off-leash crater!*

Go play, Spike!

Which one is yours?

The little double club over there. He's a purebred.
What about yours?

Ours is the purple mixed breed over there.

And...uh, I guess...

...the green one is ours too.
Tap
Tap
Tap
Tap

Hey, do you know where we can find *Trevor?*

Mr. Chuckles! No! Stay down! No jumping!
Mr. Chuckles!

I'm sorry, what was your question?
We were just wondering if you knew if *Trevor* was nearby.

Ah yes, we went to see him down at the lake last night. It's just over this hill.
Great, thanks!

Spike! Jeff! It's time to go!

Already? We just got here.

Sniff
Sniff

AAAAH

We're here,
everybody!

We're here?

Trevor is
speaking.
Let's go
listen to his
wisdom.

Do not bite the hand that feeds you.

Do not cast your pearls before swine...

Do not cry over spilled milk!

Ha
Ha Ha Ha
Ha Ha
Ha

Do not look a gift horse in the mouth or make a mountain out of a molehill...

...or count your chickens before they hatch...

...or put all your eggs in one basket!

No pain, no gain; no guts, no glory; no rest for the wicked; and no news is good news.

Ha Ha Ha Ha Ha
Ha Ha Ha Ha
Ha Ha

Fake it till you make it; fight fire with fire; first come, first served; and first things first!
Every dog has its day, every Jack has a Jill, every man has his price, and every little bit helps.

Come on, Jeff, I'll introduce you.

If it ain't broke, don't fix it; if the shoe fits, wear it; and if you can't stand the heat, then get out of the kitchen!
Trevor!

Hi, Trevor! My name is Carl. My friends and I have traveled a long distance to hear you speak.

I brought a special guest who came from *outer space* just to meet you.
He says it's his life's mission. Isn't that *neat?*

Right this way.

Jeff, I would like you to meet *Trevor...*

...our GREAT LEADER!

Live.
Laugh.
Love.

AAAAAAA

AAAAAAAAA

I have traveled light-years across the universe in a budget spaceship with no snacks and no cruise control, just to crash on the only planet of fools in the galaxy.

I might as well be conquering a culture of bacteria. No! That would actually be better because bacteria can't be stupid!
Bacteria don't stop to smell the flowers or enjoy the view or talk to fish!

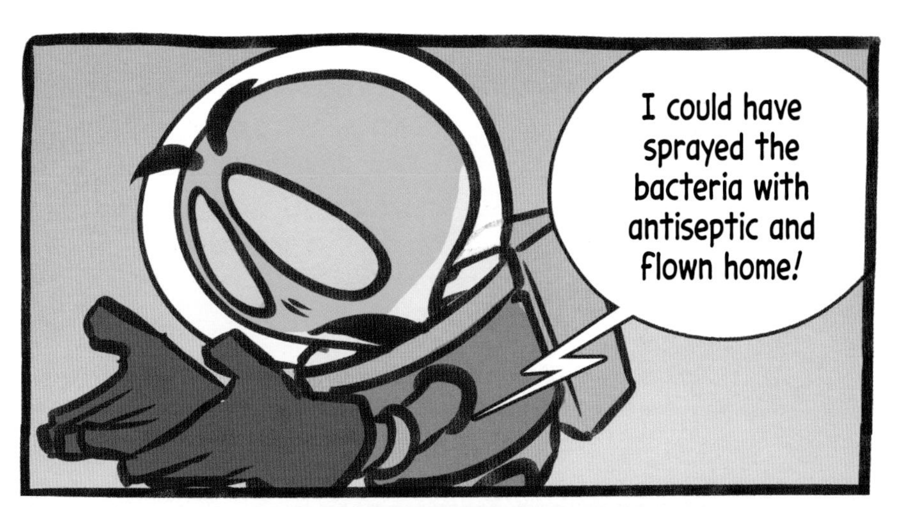
I could have sprayed the bacteria with antiseptic and flown home!

But, NOOOOOO!

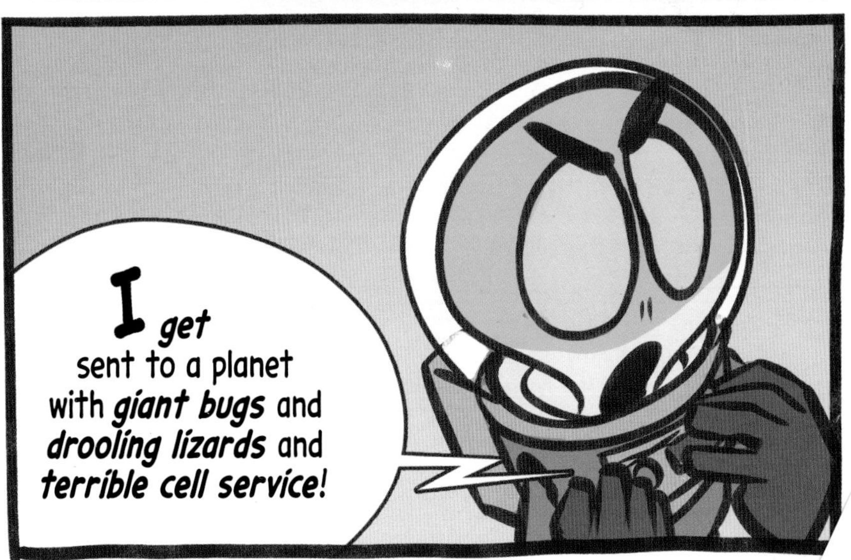
I get sent to a planet with giant bugs and drooling lizards and terrible cell service!

I *could have* been sent to planet 57-G9 with the ***chocolate volcanoes,*** or moon*7Q with the ***giant strawberries.***

But here I am on Earth, where there's just enough gravity to keep you from going anywhere fast and the mosquitoes are attracted to your breath.

...
-Click-

Thank you.
I think he's just overtired. I don't think he's angry at any of us specifically.

Oh, never mind. It looks like he's angry at you specifically.

Uh-oh, he's fogging up.
Try to settle down. Jeff, you're fogging up.

I think we should set him down under the palms to let him cool off.
Probably a good idea.

I know,
I know. There,
there.

Here you
go, a nice
cool spot.

Take your
time, friend!

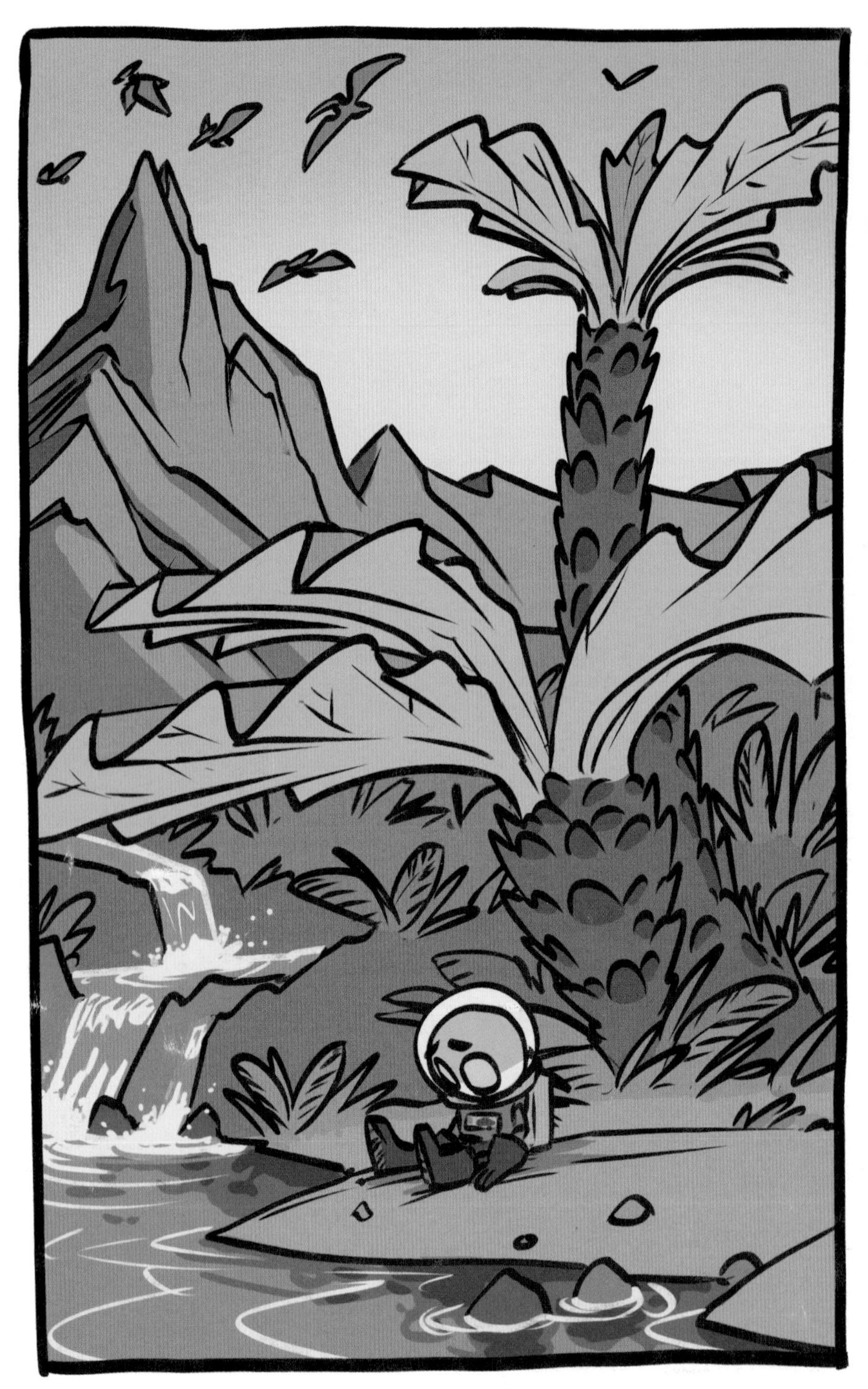

Well, hello there, strange helmeted being.

There are a lot of languages I don't speak, but I know tears when I see 'em.

You and I seem to be from different worlds, but that doesn't mean that I don't have ears to listen.

Go ahead and unload on ol' Rudy.

-Click-
I think I've been tricked.

Who tricked you?
My fellow officers.

You see, I'm not very popular on my home planet.
I don't have any real friends.
I get made fun of a lot. People at my mission base play pranks on me...

I loved being a member of the **Intergalactic Cadets.**
It was something I'd dreamed of since I was a kid.

But I soon noticed that there was a popular crowd. And I was not part of that crowd.

Sure, I got picked on a bit at first.
I thought it was just some harmless pranking.
zzZZ
WHIP
Soon I realized...

LIGHTS
GRAVITY
...I was *the only one* they picked on.

Eventually we were assigned mission base duties. Mine was *cooking.*
I learned that I loved to cook.

But it was mission pilots that were celebrated as **heroes.**

I wanted to be a hero.
Maybe then they'd stop calling me names like **Captain Kitchen...**
...and **Poopy Chef Jeff.**
Maybe I would make friends.

So I volunteered for a solo mission.
MISSION SUBMISSION

To my surprise, my mission was approved. I was being sent to conquer an entire planet by myself.
MISSION
APPROVED
I was so proud.

I was sent on a mission to conquer the third planet from star 76B.
BEAM ME UP

They told me it would be a piece of cake.

They told me the planet was inhabited with a simple little species that would bow down to me.
They told me I was going to be a ***hero*** when I returned.
They told me there were ***doughnuts*** in the spaceship.
They told me the door closed automatically like that.
They told me that Earth had great Wi-Fi.

I just wanted to make friends.

Well, it's easy to make friends on this planet! All you gotta do is *be kind* and help each other.

Then I truly *have* failed the mission.

Look here, little green man. You listen to *ol' Rudy.*

If you have failed at *conquering planets,* that is on you.
I don't know how to conquer planets, and I'm not sure you need to be good at it.

But if you fail at being a *good friend...*

...I have good news for you...
...A good friend will give you a second chance.
And all you have to do to take that second chance is say, "I need a friend like you..."

"I'm sorry."
"I'm sorry for the things I said, or the things I did, or the things I didn't do."

And, "Will you *please forgive me?*"

Sometimes your friends won't be ready to forgive you.

Be patient.

Real friendships will survive anything.

BOOM

Except that! Friendships do not survive molten lava!

Run, little green man! Go help your friends!

Thank you, Rudy!

Hungry!

Hurry, Jeff, let's go warn the others.

Wait, Hungry.
I have something
I need to say...

BA-BOOM

Can it wait?
Yup!

Carl! Dragon! Spike!
The mountain!

We know! We were just coming to get you. Let's go!

I've got Trevor!

I've got itchy toes!

Where's *Spike?*

Spike!

You guys head to higher ground. I'll get Spike!

Carl, wait!

Spike! Buddy, it's time to go. We have to leave.

Hey, let's go back to the Swamp of Despair. You can eat red ferns all day long and play in the crater...

Yip!

Okay, Spike, hang on! We'll figure this out.

Carl!

Spike!

Woo-hoo! We're on a *lava locomotion!*

Hey, Spike, wanna play *the Floor Is Lava?*

BA-BOOM

Woo-hoo!
Good boy, Spike! You saved us! Great thinking!

And just in the nick of time! We almost went over the edge of a *lavafall!*

Munch
Munch

Ah yes...
Natural selection rears its ugly head.

Aw, well, don't feel bad, Spike.

We're going to make great fossils!

ZZZZAAPT

It tickles!
Bzzt
Pop
Bzzt

Pop
Bzzt
Pop

Pop
Pop
Bzzt

Bzzt
Bzzt

Pop
Pop

Pop
Pop
Bzt

Bzz
Pop

Pop
Pop
Pop

Bzzzzzzzzzzzzzzt

Bzzzt
Bzzzt
Pop
pop

Bzzt
Bzzt
Bzzt

POP

BOOM

He did it! He saved their lives.

The battery that cleans his bubble air is empty. He needs a new battery from his ship!
Can you guys take him back there?

There they go.

You guys ready to head back to the lowlands?

Can I come?

Trevor? Don't you have more shows to perform?

I need to escape my *celebrity.* I'm tired of not being able to go out in public because of *my fame.*
I want to fit in as an average member of society. ***I just want to be a trout!***

Why don't you go back into the water?

Are you kidding? I can't swim.

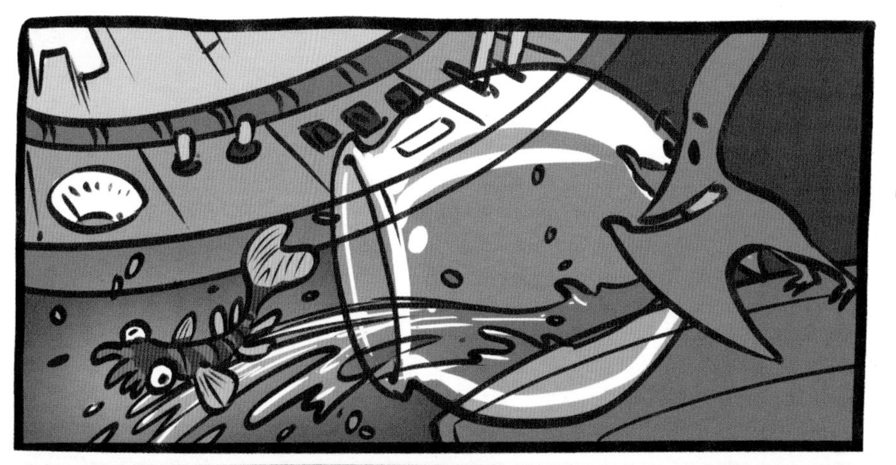

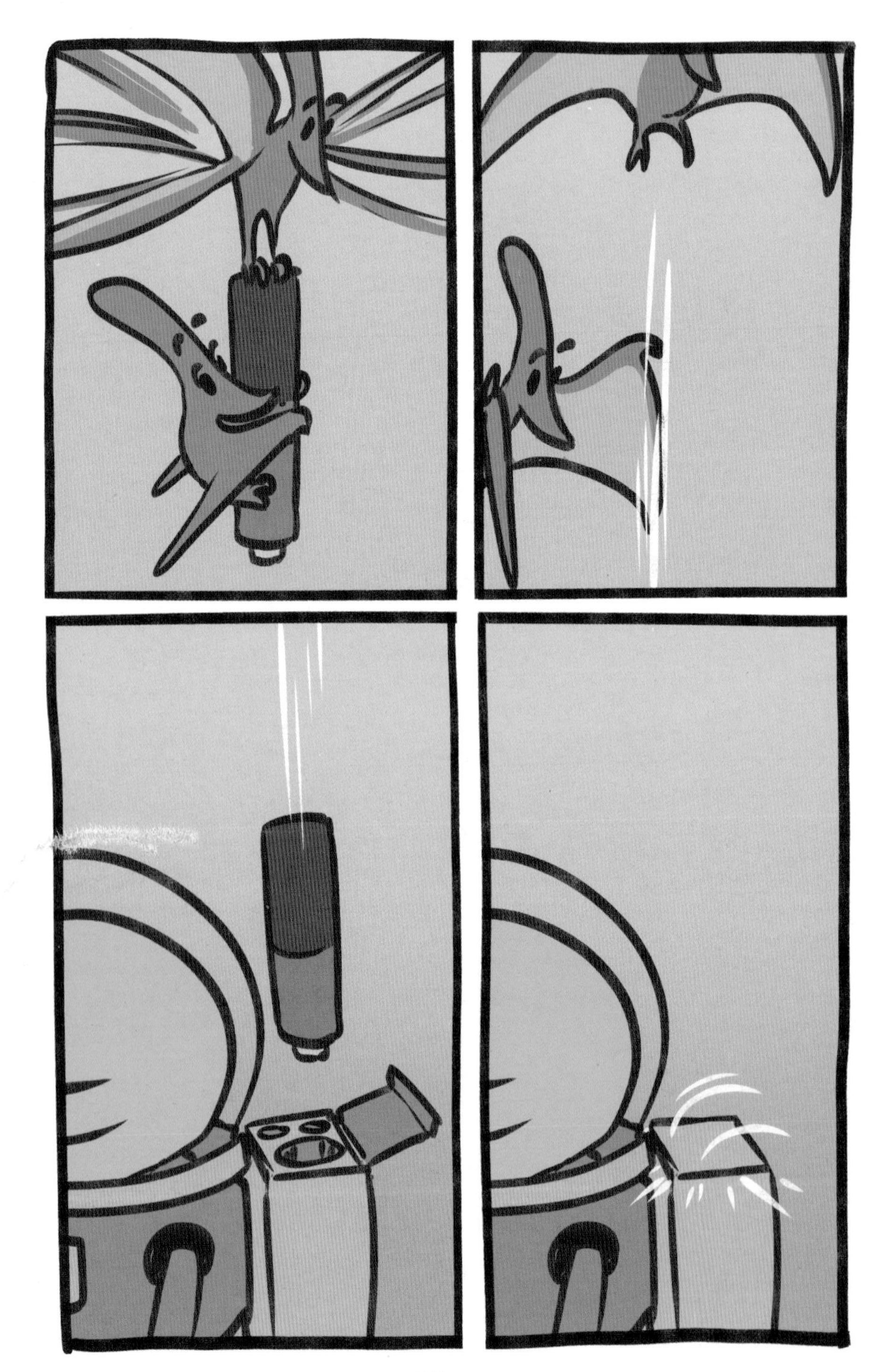

Jeff! You're okay! That was quite the display of *friendship* back there.

Actually, *the greatest* display of friendship.

Spike!

Spike, Carl, Hungry...
I need friends like you.
I'm sorry for all the times I've been *mean* and *rude* and *unhelpful.*
Please forgive me.

Aw, I forgave you a long time ago.
I forgive you, Jeff.

Yes, well, I suppose my mission to locate and overthrow the leader of this planet must be put on a temporary hold.
If I ever hope to return home, however, I *will* need to repair my ship.
And I will not be able to repair my ship unless I recover *my warp drive,* which I lost...

...somewhere over the mountains *over there.*

Sounds like we're going on a trip to the *mountains!*

Fun!

Shall we take the *scenic* route?
I would prefer to go direct.

Did anyone happen to feed my fish?

Hey, a big *grassy field!*
SWEET!

What's the deal with grassy fields?

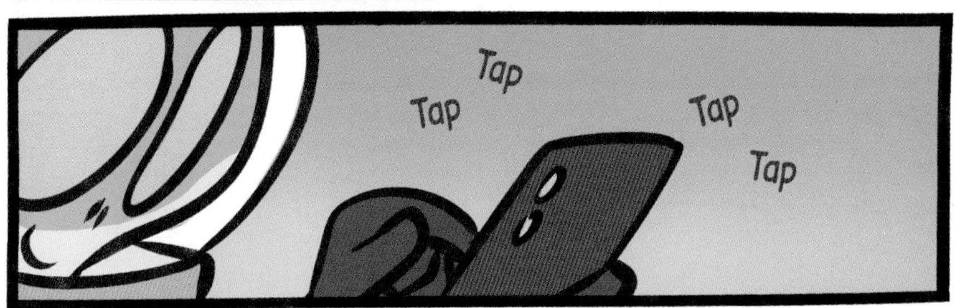
Tap
Tap
Tap
Tap

Tap

BZZZZZZAAAA

SLLLLAAARP

What was ***that?!***

It's just something we do when we visit different parts of a new planet.

You know when you go to a restaurant and you give it a rating?

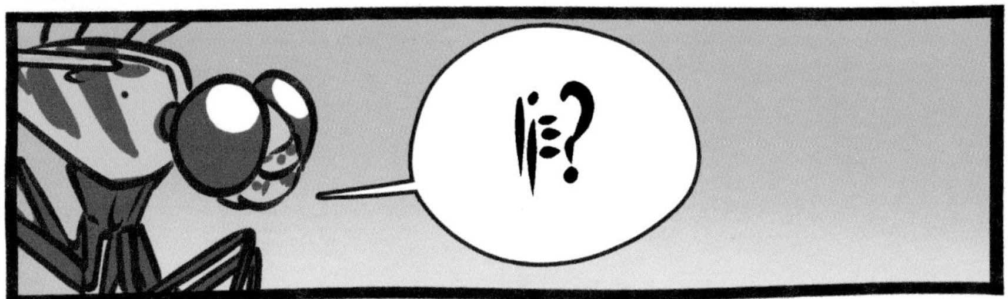

It's like telling other visitors what your experience was.

So...it's like telling other spaceship travelers that we didn't have any chicken nuggets?

Exactly!
Yeah, I want to know what he rated us too!

Well, I gave ONE star for the current state of evolution...

Fair.

See, now it seems like you're being mean again...

...***one star*** for the scenery...

It's not too late for us to take the ***scenic route.***

...one star for the food...

You are the food on this planet, Jeff.

...one star for the local guides...
...and one star for the lessons learned...

Wait...
That's *five* stars, right?
That seems pretty okay.

Some of us at the academy also like to *TAG* certain fields.

What's a *TAG?*

It's like a signature saying, "Hey, I was here!"

BZZORT
Tap

Did you just *TAG* the planet?

Sure did!

End

End?

ACKNOWLEDGMENTS

This book would not be possible without Whitney Leopard, more than an editor—someone who believed in this series. Thank you! Lillian Laserson, the best attorney I've ever Zoomed through the pandemic with! I also want to acknowledge my unofficial writers' room: Kevin Hanna and Sean Rubin, who have never met each other but have both helped me with jokes and stories, as they're both funnier people than me. And above all, my wife, Ruth, who said, "You have to do this," and then went back to work so I could focus on writing.

Thwip

How to draw Jeff

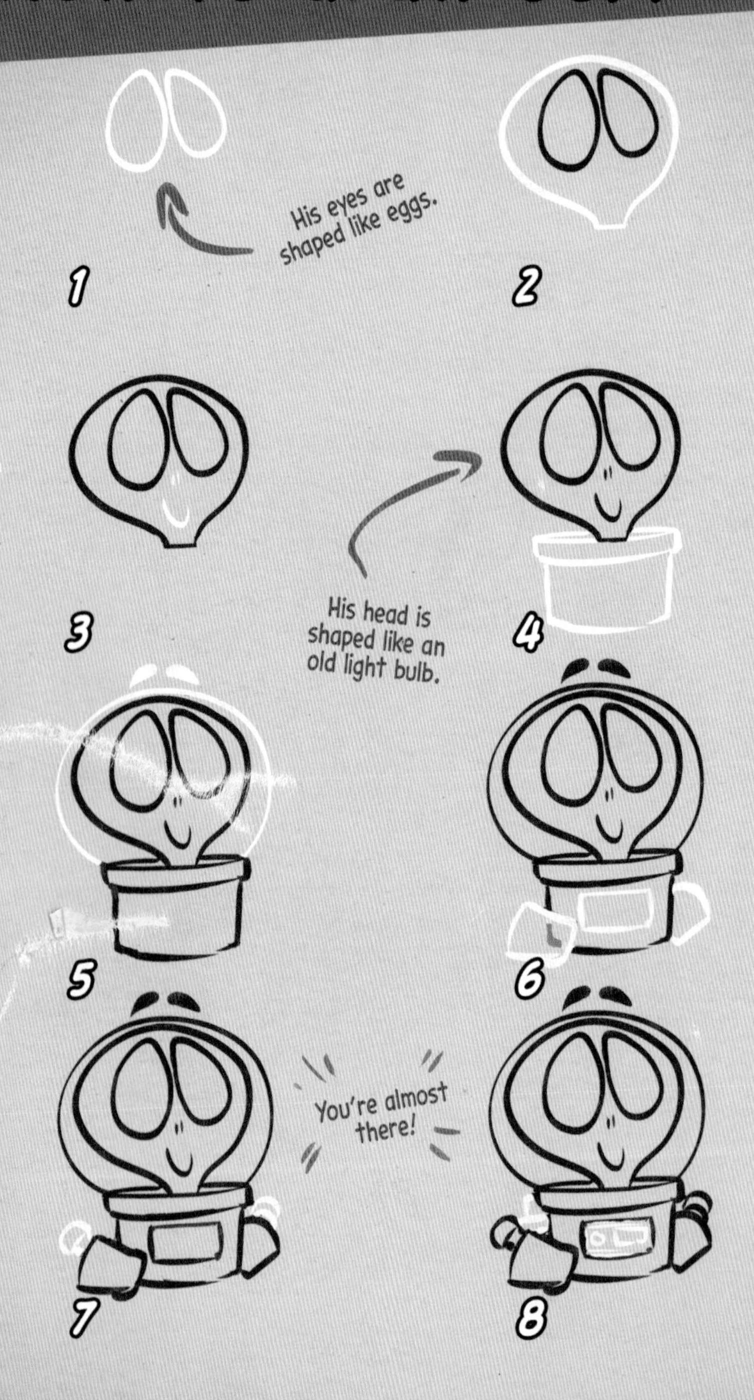

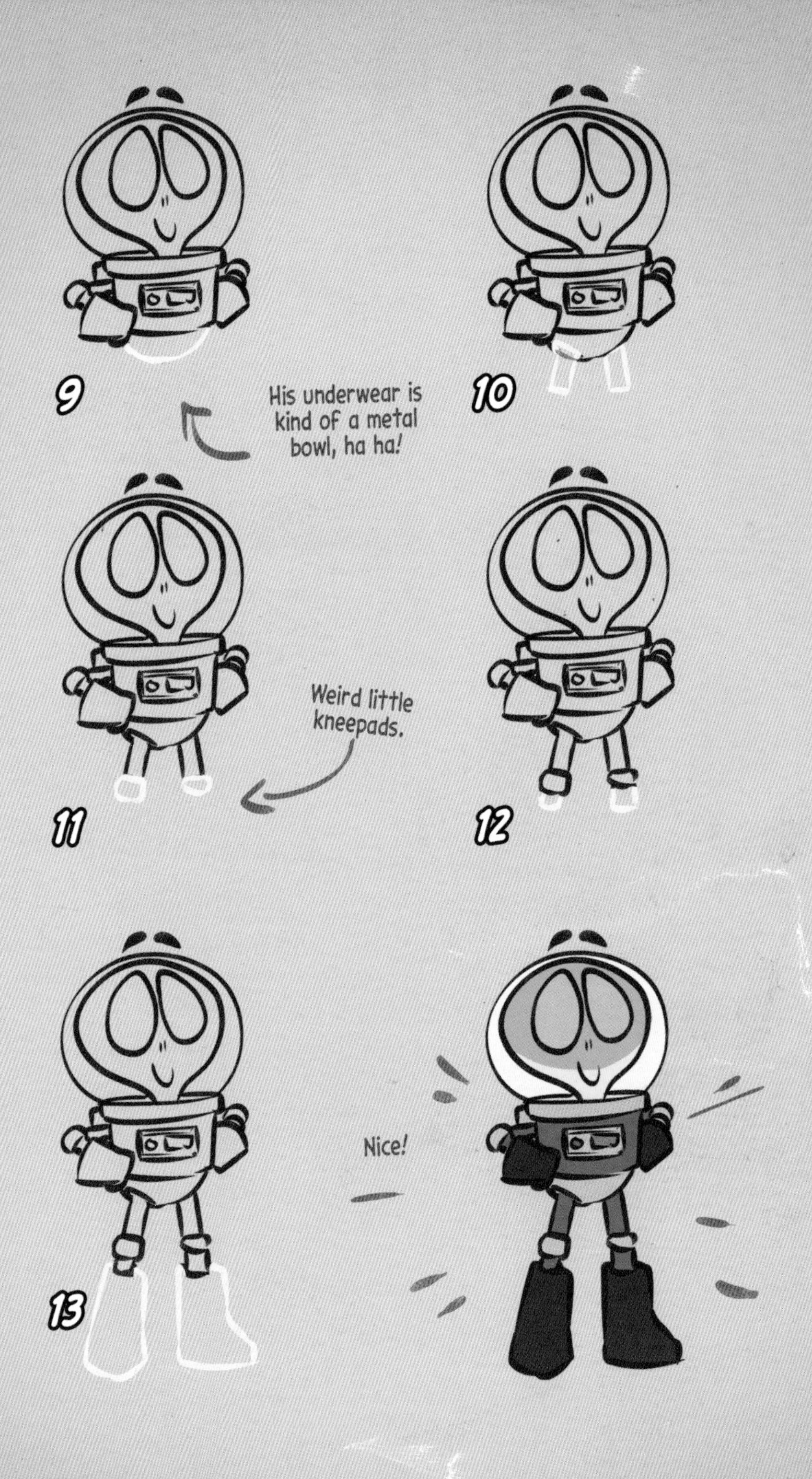
9
His underwear is kind of a metal bowl, ha ha!
10
Weird little kneepads.
11
12
13
Nice!

How to draw Carl

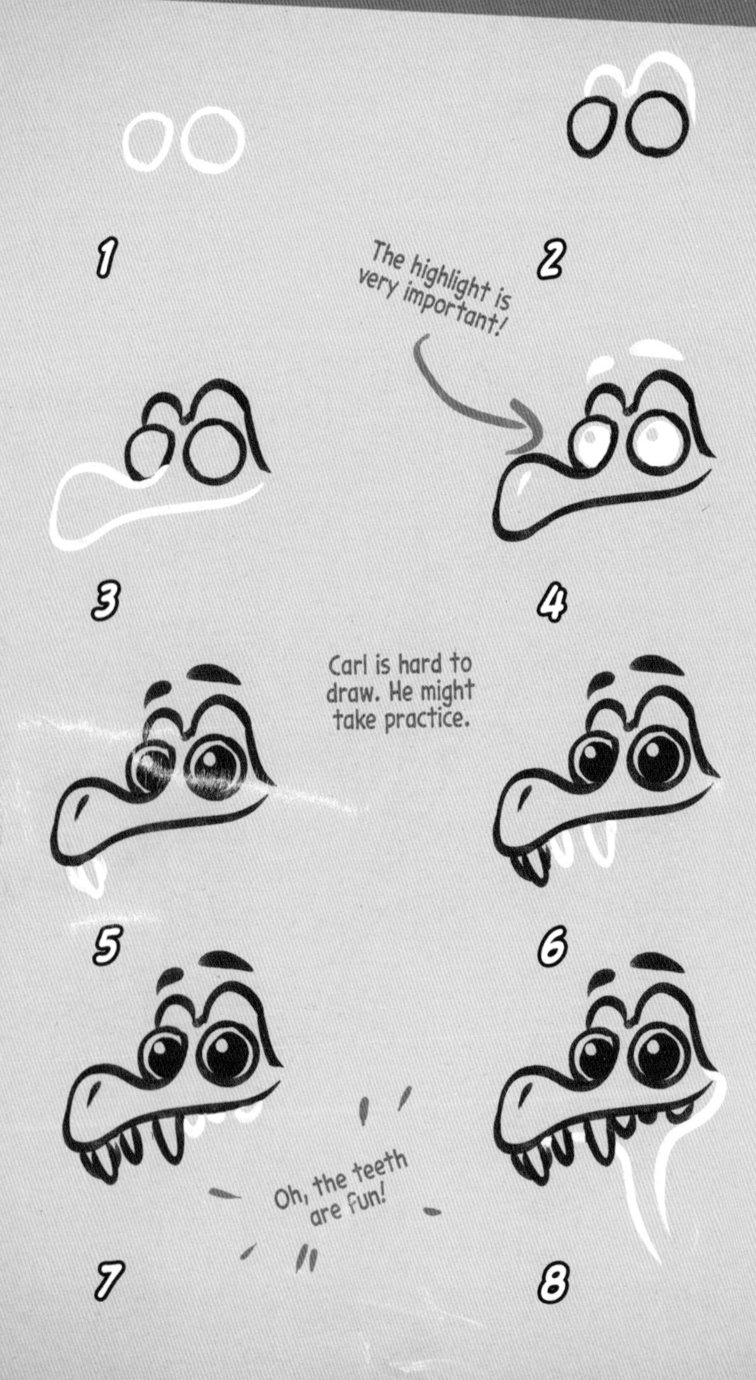

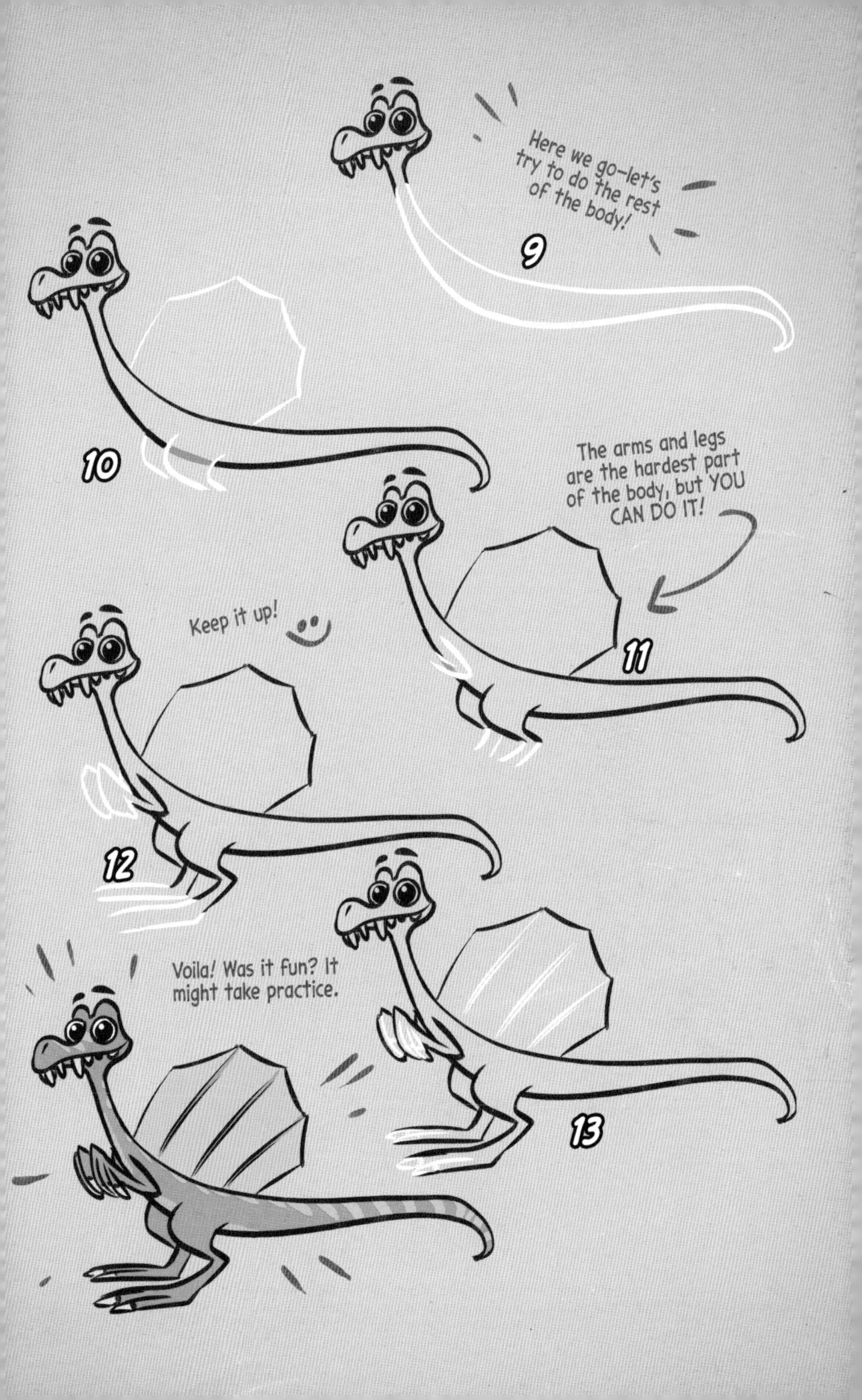
Here we go—let's try to do the rest of the body!
9
10
The arms and legs are the hardest part of the body, but YOU CAN DO IT!
11
Keep it up!
12
Voila! Was it fun? It might take practice.
13

How to write in Jeff's language

ABOUT THE CREATOR

Royden arrived on Earth at a very young age, and though there were sadly no dinosaurs, there were comic books. Hooray! Royden tried life on a farm for a few years and then moved into the forests and mountains and lived there for a few years, but now he lives in the city in Bothell, Washington. He's been drawing and writing stories for as long as he can remember. One time he got kicked out of math class for drawing in his textbook. This isn't a story about how it's okay to draw in your textbooks! One time, he failed art class because he drew comics instead of the apples on the table. Just ask your art teacher to invite Royden to do a video call with your class so you can draw comics in class too! Royden grew up to work as a video game animator, a concept artist, an art director, a photographer, and a writer and illustrator. He loves bugs and reptiles and frequently keeps them as pets. He loves drinking coffee, flying drones, and hanging out with his family. Royden is thoroughly enjoying Earth and wants to stay. On his drawing desk downstairs is his computer, his pet praying mantises, some broken drones, and a coffee cup that needs to go in the dishwasher upstairs.